This Book Belongs to:

_____

It Was Given to Me by:

_____

On This Date:

_____

# THE BIBLE AMIGOS

## FIVE LOAVES, TWO FISH, AND ONE BIG HAT

# THE BIBLE AMIGOS

## FIVE LOAVES, TWO FISH, AND ONE BIG HAT

Written and Illustrated by
Frank Fraser

SHILOH kidz
An Imprint of Barbour Publishing, Inc.

ISBN 978-1-62416-888-8

This book is a work of fiction. Names, characters, places, and incidents are either products of the author's imagination or used fictitiously. Any similarity to actual people, organizations, and/or events is purely coincidental.

Published in association with the Blythe Daniel Agency, Inc., P.O. Box 64197, Colorado Springs, CO 80962.

Published by Shiloh Kidz, an imprint of Barbour Publishing, Inc., P.O. Box 719, Uhrichsville, Ohio 44683, www.shilohkidz.com

*Our mission is to publish and distribute inspirational products offering exceptional value and biblical encouragement to the masses.*

Member of the
Evangelical Christian
Publishers Association

Printed in China.
04728 1014 SC

For Allison, Sean, and Kelly. . .

and to all the beautiful Bible Amigos found in
every corner of the world.

Keep searching, praying, and loving.

"Bible Amigos, get ready to eat!" said Donk, coming out of the kitchen with a piping hot pizza.

"That pizza's too small!" Edge complained.

"I think it's perfect," said Walla. Her compliment came with a little hug. "Sometimes, a little is enough."

During grace, Edge examined the pizza for the biggest slice. Even before the other two finished saying "Amen," Edge was diving in for *his* piece. But just as he was about to grab the biggest slice, a huge gust of wind blew the little pizza smack into his face.

"You know what that means!" said Walla, anxiously looking out the window.

"I get all the pizza?" Edge mumbled from behind the gooey mess.

"No, silly!" Walla answered, rushing outside. "That wind can only mean one thing—

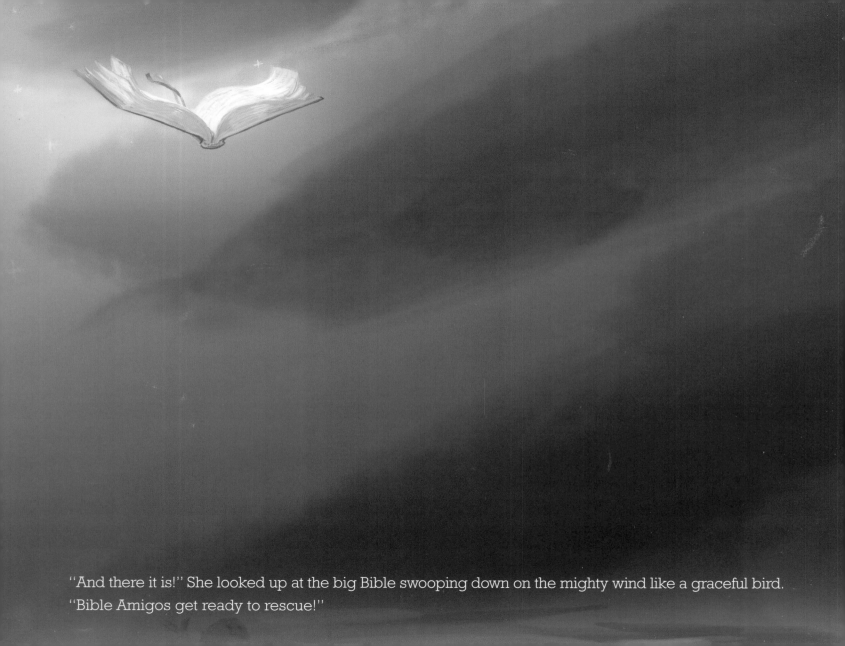

"And there it is!" She looked up at the big Bible swooping down on the mighty wind like a graceful bird. "Bible Amigos get ready to rescue!"

As they climbed aboard the giant Bible, Donk said, "I wonder where we're going."

Walla said, "I wonder who needs our help."

And Edge mumbled, "I wonder if the pizza will still be warm when I get back."

After they settled into their places, the wind lifted the Bible up into the air and the Bible Amigos cheered. . .

"Bible Amigos, go, go, go!"

And then, they were gone! gone! gone!

Meanwhile,

on the other

side of the

world. . .

Jorge begged his father, "Papa, can I work with you down in the fields today?"

"Hmmm. . . well. . .let me see." Papa knelt down. He pretended to measure Jorge. Then, with a chuckle, he said, "Even with your new big hat, you're still too little to help."

That made Jorge very unhappy. "It's not fair!" he complained, stomping down the path to the fields. "I'm not too little! I'm a big—"

## "Crocodile?!"

His complaining melted into giggles when he saw six crocodiles doing tricks on the river. "That's crazy," he laughed.

"I'll tell you what's really crazy," said Papa, shaking his head. "Driving that little boat is a tuco-tuco, and they're as blind as a bat. He probably doesn't see the bridge."

"The bridge! Watch out for the bridge!" they shouted. But the little driver could not hear them. He continued speeding right at it.

Luckily, the tuco-tuco and his little boat were so small they sailed safely under the bridge. But the crocs were not so small and not so lucky. They slammed into the bridge, sending broken boards every which way.

But crocs are tough, and the show went on. They continued down the river doing tricks as if nothing had happened. But something *did* happen; the bridge was destroyed.

Suddenly, Jorge and Papa heard someone crying, "Oh no! I hope they're going to be all right!" They spun around to find a worried mother standing behind them.

      "Oh, they're okay," Papa said calmly. "They're still doing crazy tricks down the river."

      "No, not the crocodiles. . ." she said in a shaky, little voice. "My *children*—across the river!

"I came across the river to get food for my children, and now the bridge is broken. . . I can't get back to them!"

Papa reassured her. "Don't worry. I'll go down and see what I can do."

"And I'll help!" said Jorge, taking a giant step toward the broken bridge.

But Papa's arm was longer than Jorge's eager step. "Jorge, you are too little to build a bridge. Stay here and don't get overheated. The sun is really hot."

Jorge felt that familiar grumbling
feeling churning around inside him.
He heard the men making their plans
down by the broken bridge.

"We'll need a big tractor."
"Big spools of rope."
"Ten more men."
"At least a hundred new wood planks."
"And a couple of days to fix this, especially in this heat."

With each suggestion, Jorge grumbled and he grumbled some more. He was so wrapped up in his little self
that he didn't notice that the mother was crying. . .until she turned her head and looked sadly across the river

toward her children. When Jorge saw that, he felt more sorry for her than he did for himself. "If only I were big, I could help you. But I'm not." He pulled his big hat down over his face. "I'm little, and there's nothing I can do."

Just then, Jorge felt a big wind nearly lift him up. Someone giggled, "Hello! Are you trapped in your big hat?"

When he looked up from under his hat, he saw the giant Bible and the three Bible Amigos coming toward him. "Who are you?" he asked.

"We're the Bible Amigos and we're here to help."
    "Well, *I* don't need help," said Jorge. "But *she* sure does." Jorge told the whole story about how the bridge was broken and how the mother couldn't get to her children across the river.

"That is a problem," said Edge. "But, it looks like the men are already working on fixing the bridge. Soooo. . ."—he scratched his prickly chin—"what are *you* doing to help this mother?"

Jorge shrugged, "I'm little; what *can* I do?"

*"What can you do?* That's a great question!" Walla ran and gave the big Bible a big hug. "Lucky for you, and the whole world, God put every answer to every important question right here in the Bible."

Edge lifted the brim of Jorge's hat and looked him straight in the eyes. "So you think just because you're little, you can't do big things?"

Jorge shrugged.

"Would you like to see what God has to say about that?"

Jorge did, but there were so many pages in the Bible. "How will we know where to look for the answer?" he asked.

Donk began turning the giant pages. "If you're really, honestly looking for answers, God kinda makes 'em pop out at you." He kept turning pages until. . .

"Ta-da!
This looks like it," said
Walla. "Thank you, Bible,
we'll take it from here.
A long time ago. . ."

John 6:1-14

how will you believe my words?

. . .a super big crowd followed Jesus way out to the countryside to hear Him talk about all the Good News He brought, like how much God loves each of us and other awesome things like that.

But the sun was going down,
and no one had brought any food. Since Jesus
never wants anybody to be hungry, He asked
his friend Philip, "Where shall we buy bread for
these people to eat?"
Philip said even if there were someplace
nearby, there was no way they'd have
enough money to buy food for
5,000 people.

Then Andrew, one of Jesus' other friends, blurted out, "Hey, here is a little boy with five loaves of bread and two small fish!" Andrew might not have believed that was enough to feed 5,000 hungry people, but it was the best he could come up with.

But the little boy didn't see the problem the same way the big men did. He loved Jesus so much, he didn't think about what he could or couldn't do. He simply said, "Jesus, I only have a little, but I am happy to give it all to You." And that made Jesus happy.

After blessing the food, Jesus told His friends to give the boy's gift of bread and fish to the crowd.

nothing may be lost.

...rophet who is to come into t...

It didn't make sense to Jesus' friends. There were 5,000 hungry people and only five loaves of bread. But the men trusted Jesus, and they did what He asked. They handed out the bread and fish. And when they should have run out of food, they discovered that more was in the basket! Jesus kept reaching in and pulling out more food until everybody ate as much as they wanted.

And when they collected the leftovers, they filled up twelve more baskets! They had started out with just five loaves of bread and two fish, and after everyone was fed they ended up with about ten times as much.

Of course, the crowd was amazed. They praised God because they saw how much Jesus could do with so little, especially when it was given with love.

"The End."

"Wow!" said Jorge. "Jesus fed all those people with just five loaves of bread and two small fish? That's awesome! But what this mother needs is a *bridge*. All I have is a big hat, and a big hat is not going to fix a bridge."

"Remember five loaves of bread wasn't going to feed 5,000 people either," said Edge. "Jesus asked for help to point out something very important: He wants us to remember we can't do things alone. We always need His help. Jesus wants us to give all that we can with love and trust that He can do a lot with a little."

Jorge looked up toward the sky. "Jesus," he said, "I sure do want to help this mother, but I don't know what to do." Then he looked at the mother who sat so uncomfortably in the heat. Suddenly, he grinned a grin so big that it could barely fit under his hat. "I know it's not much," he said, "but it's all I've got." He took off his big hat and placed it gently on the mother's head. "At least, in this very hot sun, I can give you shade with my very big hat."

The mother stood up to give Jorge a hug, and then something amazing happened.

A mighty wind came out of nowhere blowing the hat *and* the mother into the river.

"Oh no!" shouted Jorge. But he was quickly relieved when he saw that the mother was floating safely across the river to her children. "Thank You, Jesus!" said Jorge. "You really *can* do a lot with a little."

He turned to thank the Bible Amigos and tell them that they were right. . .
but they were already on their way. As they flew past Jorge, Edge tossed him
a Bible with a little note that read:

# The End

*God has more to tell you about this in the Bible;
here are some of our favorite passages:*

*Walla's favorite: Luke 1:37*

*Donk's favorite: 1 John 3:18*

*Edge's favorite: Matthew 13:31–32*

*Edge's other favorite: Isaiah 60:22*

God said, "Draw." Frank did, and has never stopped.

God said, "Marry Terri." Frank did, and would do it again.

God said, "Have kids." Frank (and Terri) did: three.

Frank doesn't know what God told them, but he now has nine grandchildren.

God said, "Move to Texas." Frank said, "Huh?"

But that is where he and Terri now live, and where he now draws.